Lying Around

by Anna Prokos

illustrated by Diane Greenseid

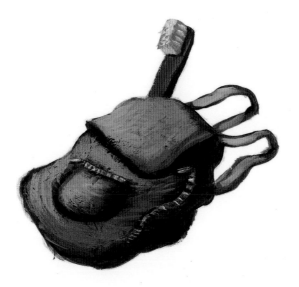

RED
CHAIR
·PRESS·

Leon the lion is prowling around.
He finds some items in the grass.
Leon hides them in his backpack.

He strolls toward the river.
"A perfect spot to lie around," he says.

Mac the macaw is flying around.
He is looking for something.
"Achoo! I've lost my tissues," Mac says.
"Have you seen them?"

Leon shakes his head.
"I haven't seen anything," Leon lies.
Mac scratches his beak then flies away.

Kyle the crocodile is crawling around.
He is looking for something.
"I've lost my toothbrush," Kyle says.
"Have you seen it?"

Leon shakes his head.
"I haven't seen anything,"
Leon lies again.
Kyle crawls away.

Rita the cheetah is stalking around.
She is looking for something.
"I've lost a sneaker," Rita tells Leon.
"Have you seen it?"

Leon shakes his head.
"I haven't seen anything," he lies for
a third time. Rita walks away.

"I'm bored with lying around," Leon yawns.
So up he jumps, and SPLASH!
Leon falls into the river.

Mac, Kyle, and Rita race to the rescue. What do they see?

"My tissues!" Mac squawks.
"My toothbrush!" Kyle chomps.
"My sneaker!" Rita remarks.

"I don't know how these got here," Leon lies.
"I've been lying around all day."
"You have been lying all day," Mac caws.
"And now you're in trouble!"

Lying Leon turns bright red.
"I'm sorry I lied," he says.
"I promise I won't do it again."
Mac, Kyle, and Rita help Leon
out of the water.

"Now I can get back to what lions
do best," Leon says. "Lying around!"
"We'll help too," say all his friends.
And they do.

Big Question: What lesson did Leon learn about lying? Did his friends forgive him?

Big Words:

crawling: move slowly along the ground

prowling: move around in search of something

rescue: save from being lost

stalking: move silently in search of something